Selznick, Brian.

The robot king.

DATE			

BAKER & TAYLOR

The
ROBOT KING

The
ROBOT
KING

Brian Selznick

A LAURA GERINGER BOOK
An Imprint of HarperCollins*Publishers*

Library of Congress Cataloging-in-Publication Data

Selznick, Brian.

   The robot king / by Brian Selznick.

      p.   cm.

   Summary: Two motherless children build a robot from odds and ends in their attic and, by using their mother's favorite belonging as its heart, bring the creation to life.

   ISBN 0-06-024493-3. — ISBN 0-06-024494-1 (lib. bdg.)

   [1. Robots—Fiction.   2. Brothers and sisters—Fiction.

   3. Magic—Fiction.]   I. Title.

PZ7.S4654Ro   1995   94-43808

[Fic]—dc20   CIP

                                           AC

Typography by Christine Kettner

1 2 3 4 5 6 7 8 9 10

❖

First Edition

For Joe Rubin
and
Monica Landry

ONE

ZRA WAS FILLING his pockets
again with tiny stones and whatever lost
things he could find in the grass. Lucy sat
nearby arranging some flowers in a circle on
the ground. She picked up a small piece of
glass, examined it in the moonlight, and
handed it to Ezra. He smiled and buried it
in his pocket.

From where they sat, a distant streetlamp

outlined the gravestone with light. It reminded Lucy of the way their mother's hair would glow as she brought them up to bed, with a candle to light the dark stairs.

Lucy remembered very little about their mother. She remembered music and rain and the smell of lightning. Only that, and the candle on the stairs. So Lucy made up stories about her, with great lightning storms and adventures. She sat leaning against the gravestone, telling the stories to Ezra, who made little teepees out of sticks and set them in the ground. He had decided he couldn't remember their mother at all.

When it was time to go, Lucy told Ezra to clear the grass. He picked up his teepees and put them in his pocket. He brushed away the leaves, being careful not to disturb the circle of flowers that Lucy had arranged.

Lucy wiped the gravestone clean with the bottom of her dress. Then they stood up, and she brushed the dirt from their clothing, turning for a moment toward the old fairgrounds, which rose up behind the graveyard and stood against the sky like dinosaur skeletons. Wind whistled through the broken carousel, and its flying animals waited silently beneath the stars.

As she stared at the dark outline of the Ferris wheel and the cracked backbone of the roller coaster, Lucy made up another story for Ezra. In the story, Ezra was a little baby, and Lucy carried him through the fairgrounds with their mother and father. There were fireworks and lights that were so bright they had to cover their eyes. The carousel spun them around and the Ferris wheel lifted them high into the night sky. When

Lucy finished her story, the children turned again and walked toward home.

All along the way, Ezra stopped to pick things up that were glinting in the darkness. He filled his pockets until he could hardly move his legs. Patiently, Lucy waited for him, pulling aside branches and helping him carry whatever he couldn't manage himself. It was a long walk back.

When they finally reached home they let themselves silently in so Aunt Violet wouldn't know they had gone off to the graveyard again. Without ever making a sound, they passed the back parlor where she sat brooding over the giant wooden puzzle she had been working on ever since she arrived. Aunt Violet didn't think attics and graveyards were proper places for the children. But she resigned herself to leaving them to their own devices, since their father would be returning soon.

Up in the attic, Ezra unloaded his pockets onto the floor. He immediately began separating everything into smaller piles, organizing his treasures. Ezra's collection was huge and everything had its place: chips of blue glass went into one jar, green into another. There was a box for pieces of toy soldiers, and he catalogued the pebbles from the graveyard by color and size and kept them in five dusty shoe boxes under a table. Glass jars, some filled with twigs and some with silverware, balanced on one of the sagging windowsills, cans of lost keys were jammed between books, and in the corner there was a big round dish overflowing with buttons.

Ezra loved to take things apart. He had an assortment of clockworks, wires, and springs that were secretly taken from appliances downstairs. Clocks or lamps would mysteriously stop working, and when their father got rid of them, Ezra would sneak them upstairs, where they would eventually end up in a hundred tiny pieces.

Because he had no choice, Ezra let Lucy go through his vast collections. He allowed her to keep whatever she wanted. Out of these odd bits and pieces, she made mechanical toys. She made a car that walked like an insect out of twigs, spoons, and metal pipes. She attached wheels and wind-up engines to a fleet of china doll heads which she raced across the attic. She built a rocket ship that spun and made sparks when you turned the

key. Ezra, who once was bitten by Lucy's wind-up boat, stayed as far away as possible from everything she made.

Ezra was taking apart one of his broken clocks, piece by piece, when Lucy snuck up behind him. "Come downstairs with me," she whispered.

Ezra did not like how this sounded so he didn't look up.

"I need some things from mother's old room. Father's away and he'll never know. *Please*, Ezra, I don't want to go alone."

Ezra continued to fiddle with the clock.

"Listen to me, Ezra. Don't you want to know what I'm building now? Don't shake your head, you do! This is not like the other things, you know . . . It's not a toy." Lucy paused for a moment. "It needs something of *mother's.* I remember . . . there's a music box . . ."

Ezra looked up at her quickly and they stared at each other.

"Please, Ezra," Lucy said again. "I want it."

Very slowly, Ezra got up and walked across the attic. He dragged a table over to the wall, put a chair on the table, and climbed up. From above a rafter that stretched across the attic, Ezra produced a large carton that Lucy had never seen before.

Dust swirled up out of the box as he reached inside. Lucy watched as Ezra slowly pulled out their mother's music box. Carefully he handed it to Lucy. It was covered with rust. She cradled it in her hands. "Ezra, you shouldn't have gone into her room," Lucy whispered. "You could have gotten caught."

Ezra unpacked the rest of the box. There

were books and rings and two little porcelain sculptures, a hairbrush, and a mirror. There was a small framed photograph, and there were pearls and a brass candle holder.

The two children looked at everything on the table for a long time. Lucy picked up the framed photograph, a ring, the hairbrush, the mirror, and the candle holder. She nodded to Ezra, and he gently returned everything else to its hiding place. Lucy took a deep breath. "Now we can finish," she said. "Come with me!"

Ezra shook his head.

"Come with me!" She led Ezra across the attic to where she was working. Something large was lying on a table beneath a cloth. Ezra did not want to look at it.

"Look!" Lucy said as she pulled off the cloth.

It was wearing a red velvet coat and a blue bow tie. Lucy attached the framed photograph to its stomach with wires and slid the ring onto a fork that stuck out of its leg. She pushed the hairbrush, the mirror, and the candle holder under some wires beneath its coat.

"You can wind up the heart," Lucy said.

Ezra didn't understand what she meant until she handed him the music box. His hands were shaking, but he wound it until the little knob wouldn't turn anymore. It didn't make a sound.

"Doesn't matter," Lucy said. "Now give it to me."

Ezra did as he was told and backed away.

"Don't worry, Ezra, there's nothing to be afraid of, nothing at all. He won't bite you, I promise."

She forced open a space between two

18

pieces of metal and slipped the music box into place like a surgeon. She covered and tied everything back over it. "There!" she cried triumphantly, "We're finished. You can open your eyes now. Are you okay?"

Ezra nodded.

She straightened the crooked bow tie and pulled the velvet sleeves so they were even. She checked the china plate knees to make sure they were still on straight. "Even if the world was filled with robots," she said, "*he* would still be king." Lucy looked at her brother. "Ezra, say hello to the Robot King!"

Of course Ezra did not say anything. He didn't move.

And the Robot King remained perfectly still.

Perfectly.

And silent.

But suddenly the broken music box started playing by itself! The children grabbed each other and stepped back. With a great heave, the Robot King's chest began to rise and fall, and his fingers started moving and he shivered to his toes and *BOOM! He opened his eyes!*

Lucy screamed as the attic burst with light. The Robot King's electric body threw off golden sparks that filled the air like fireworks.

"Oh!" cried Lucy. "He's alive, Ezra! He's alive!"

The Robot King inhaled deeply. "He's shaking all over," said Lucy, "Help me sit him up. Take his hand, Ezra. . . . Take it!"

So Lucy and Ezra held the Robot King's hands, and when they touched him for the first time, a thrilling shock raced up their arms. The Robot King stopped shaking as the children helped him sit up. "You can let go of him now," Lucy said. "I've got him. Ezra? Let go!"

But Ezra wouldn't let go. He held the Robot King's hand and smiled.

"Oh, look!" Lucy said, "He's moving his head. Hello! Hello!" She touched the Robot King's face. "I'm Lucy and this is Ezra. You're the Robot King. Do you hear a waltz? That's your heartbeat, and this is the attic where—Oh no! Stop!"

The Robot King was leaning forward. He was inching himself off the table.

Before the children could stop him he came toppling down and fell straight to the floor, crashing to his knees, which shattered into a thousand pieces. Then he fell the rest of the way with a loud horrible bang.

"No!" Lucy cried, "Please don't be broken!" The children rolled the Robot King onto his back. The waltz was still rising from his chest. Lucy leaned her face close, squeezed his shoulders, and sighed with relief. She brushed the dust and china pieces off the Robot King's jacket. The children looked at the sea of broken knees around them. "It's alright," Lucy said to the Robot King as they sat him up. "We can fix this." Ezra got two more plates out of a box in the corner of the attic and gave them to Lucy. She snapped the new knees on and made sure that they were even.

Ezra picked up all the broken pieces of the Robot King's knees and poured them into an empty jar. Quickly he screwed a lid onto the jar and set it on the windowsill, hurrying back to help Lucy.

If Ezra had stayed at the window one more moment he would have seen that the ledge was uneven. He would have seen the jar topple backwards, out the window, and he would have seen what happened next.

The jar crashed to the ground, and when it broke, all the pieces of the Robot King's knees were set free. Immediately they picked themselves up and flew away into the sky, up and up and shining like a swarm of porcelain bees. They flashed in the moonlight and were gone.

Lucy and Ezra helped the Robot King stand, holding him tightly as he slowly unbent his back and straightened his legs.

The children held him steady and were afraid to move in case the Robot King should fall again. So the three of them just stood there, together.

Suddenly the Robot King's left foot slid forward. The children gasped and grabbed him tighter. Then he slid his right foot forward, dragging the children with him. He moved his left foot again, and then his right. "He's walking!" Lucy shouted. "Ezra, he's walking! Don't let go!"

They led the Robot King around the

crowded attic, stepping between tables and boxes and cluttered piles. They stopped by the window. The Robot King turned to look outside, but Lucy leaned over and closed the curtains. She stood in front of him and carefully let go.

Ezra held on tightly to the Robot King.

"Go on, Ezra, let go," Lucy said.

So Ezra did. The Robot King stood by himself. The children stepped back a little. "Come to me," Lucy said. She put out her hands. The Robot King looked at Ezra. Then he looked at Lucy. Slowly he took his first steps by himself. One foot, and then the other until he was in Lucy's arms again. "Lucy! Ezra! Time for bed!" came the call from downstairs.

Lucy laid the Robot King down on the

table and fixed his crooked bow tie while Ezra straightened out the jacket. The children's fingers tingled just from touching him.

"'night," whispered Lucy. "Say good night, Ezra." But Ezra just touched the Robot King's chest and held his hand there, watching it rise and fall. The metal vibrated against his palm. "You know, Ezra, sometimes I wish you'd talk," Lucy whispered. "I know you still *can* because you talk in your sleep and I hear you. Ezra? Are you listening to me?" Ezra slowly shook his head. He kept staring at the Robot King. "It's okay," Lucy said, "come on." She took Ezra's hand. "We both say good night," she said to the Robot King. Then she turned out the lights and opened the attic door, locking it behind her as they headed down to sleep.

In the middle of the night a fly flew in the window and started buzzing all around the Robot King. It slammed into his head, backed off, and dove right in again. Buzzzzzz clink! The Robot King sat up, stretched out his arm, and caught the fly in midair. It buzzed like wildfire in his hand until it settled down and rested. The Robot King opened his fingers just long enough to see that it wasn't a fly at all, but a small stray piece of his broken knee. And whooosh! It was gone, flying away into the darkness.

☆

The next day, the children found the

Robot King standing near the wall, examining a broken clock. He bent his head close and tapped the clock in his hand. "Good morning," Lucy said. "That's a clock. It tells you what time it is, but this one's broken." The Robot King held the clock near his face. He turned it around and around. He poked his finger into the clock and something snapped. The Robot King tried to pull his finger out, but he couldn't. It was stuck.

The children tried to pull the clock off but it wouldn't budge. They let go, and the Robot King shook his finger back and forth. Nothing worked, so he left the clock where it was.

He walked over to a shelf and picked up an open can of nails. The Robot King shook the can, brought it close to his face, and turned it over. All the nails fell out and clattered against the floor. The Robot King looked at Lucy. "Those are nails," she said. The Robot King stepped over the nails on the floor, turned around, and walked over to Lucy's rolling doll heads. Lucy wound up seven or eight of them. "We can have races," she said. She set them on the ground and they rattled across the attic, spinning in circles as they went. One of them bumped into Ezra, who was picking up the nails. He shooed it away quickly like a mouse.

Lucy turned to the Robot King. "How are we going to get that clock off of you," she wondered aloud. "Ezra, get your tools, but be careful. Don't hurt his finger." Ezra put the nails away and got his screwdriver. He held the Robot King's hand to inspect the clock. The Robot King reached up with his other hand and touched Ezra's face, gently bringing his fingertips over Ezra's eyes and mouth. He moved Ezra's nose from side to side, and then he felt his own nose. Lucy moved closer and the Robot King examined her hair. He lifted Lucy's hand and tested each of her fingers. "Let Ezra take the clock off your finger," Lucy said.

The Robot King waved the clock on the end of his finger. Then he got up and walked over to the window. He stood there with his back to the children. There was a slight breeze and the curtains opened up and wrapped themselves around the Robot King like arms. He pointed out the window. Lucy hesitated, then quietly said, "That's the sky." She came up behind him and closed the curtains.

The Robot King drew apart the curtains and pointed again. The clock scraped across the window frame. "That's enough," Lucy said, "Those are trees and streetlamps. That's a road. Now please let me close the curtains."

But as soon as they were closed, the Robot King opened them again. Lucy held his hand. "That's outside, where you get lost," she said. "Here in the attic, everything is ours! Look! Trees and streetlamps . . ." She pointed to a hat rack capped with top hats and a lightbulb hanging from a wire. "A road . . ." she said, and she pointed to the path between some boxes. "The sky . . . ," and she pointed to the crisscrossed wood that ran across the ceiling. "The world!"

"Come, Ezra," Lucy called, "Let's travel around the world!"

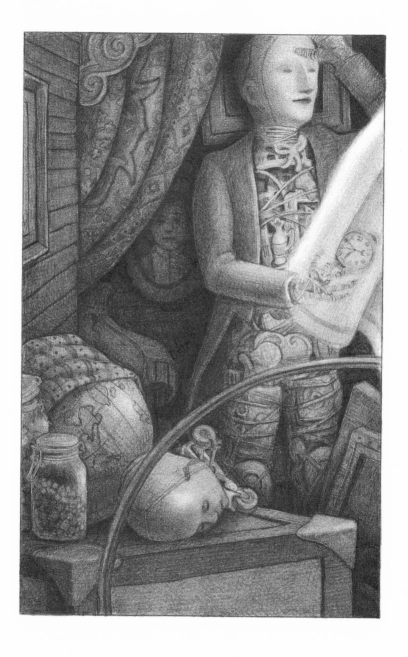

So they set out, voyaging into the four far corners of the attic. The lightbulb streetlamp swayed gently above them as they made their way down the attic road, around the attic tree, beneath the attic sky.

✶

Midway through the night, long after the children had finally gone to bed, the knee came back, snuck up behind the Robot King, and smacked into his head. It zipped through the air trying to avoid his hands when *crash!* The Robot King hit the little piece of porcelain with the clock. It shattered into several smaller pieces that were hurled across the attic. They hit the wall and fell to the ground, in a cluttered pile of broken things.

One landed in an old radio, one in a crushed lamp, and the third piece ended up in a rusty telephone.

There was a faint electric hum, and then, one by one, the radio, the lamp, and the telephone lifted themselves up into the air and flew around the Robot King. The crackled voice of a woman singing in Italian came out of the radio, the lamp turned bright and dark and bright again, and the phone rang. The Robot King tried to grab the telephone, but he kept knocking himself in the head with the clock that was stuck on his finger. He stopped for a moment and tried once again to pull the clock off. He pulled as hard as he could, heard a loud *crack*, and watched as the clock came flying off his finger. Instead of falling to the ground though, it flung itself higher into the air, tick-tocking and spinning its arms in perfect time.

The Robot King raised his arm and saw that the end of his finger had come off inside the clock. He watched all the machines turning in the air around him, and then he looked down and searched through Ezra's collection. He found a broken toy train, picked it up, and threw it into the air. Immediately it fell, crashing loudly to the ground. The Robot King bent over, unscrewed one of his toes, and put it into the train. He threw it into the air again. It started to fall, but suddenly its little engine revved up, its tiny smokestack blew tiny plumes of smoke, and its wheels and pistons started turning. It climbed through the air on steely invisible tracks, circling higher and higher. The radio, the lamp, the telephone, and the clock, all led by the train, turned and flew out the window.

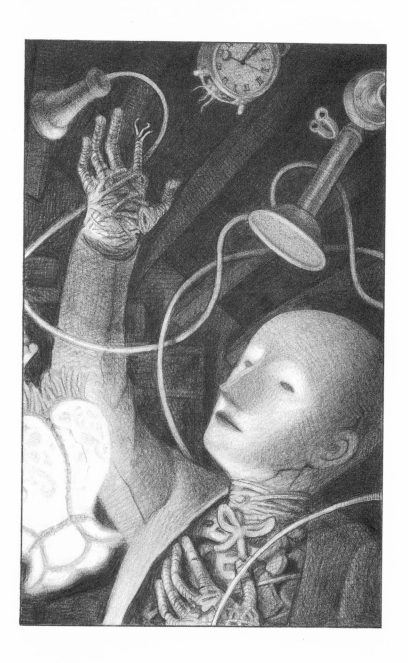

The Robot King watched as they rose into the sky and vanished.

☆

The next day the Robot King sat the children down in front of him. "What happened?" Lucy cried. "The clock came off your finger! Oh no! Your finger's broken! Where's the rest of your finger?" The Robot King was holding an old broken pocket watch, and he answered her by bending over and unscrewing another toe. "What are you doing?" Lucy cried. "Stop it! Put your toe back on this minute!"

But the Robot King put his toe inside the pocket watch, snapped the cover shut, and handed it to Lucy. It began ticking. Then it jumped up into the air and floated above her palm.

"Look, Ezra," she said in awe as she passed the watch to him. He pushed it lightly with his finger and it came back. He pushed it again and it came back again.

Lucy got up and hugged the Robot King. She led him to a table where she sat him down. She studied the frayed wires at the end of his finger and where his toe used to be. "You're missing *two* toes! What have you been doing?" She shook her head. "Now stay still," she said. "I'm going to make you a new fingertip and some new toes, but only this once." She turned around to get some supplies from Ezra's glass jars on a bookcase behind her. She pulled out some wires and reached up to the top shelf to get some scraps of tin. She stood on her tiptoes, but she was too short. She reached as high as she could when all of a sudden she felt herself being lifted off the ground. She looked down and saw the Robot King holding her in midair. She easily got what she needed from the top shelf and the Robot King brought her gently back to the ground. "Thank you," Lucy said.

She sat him down at the table again and held his hand in hers. The Robot King watched carefully as Lucy fashioned the new toes and a fingertip for him out of the bits of tin and strands of wire.

"What you did with your toe was . . . incredible," she said. "It was a miracle. But . . . you may never do it again! Do you understand? You can not take yourself apart!"

The Robot King stood up and Lucy put her arms around him again. Ezra slipped in

between them, stepping up onto the Robot King's feet. The three of them stood with their arms around each other. Lucy held her ear to the Robot King's body. She closed her eyes and saw the music box in their mother's room, the way it was a long time ago.

The three of them began to move. They rocked a little at first, but then they took a step. And then another. And another. Lucy held on to the Robot King, who carried Ezra between them, on his feet. The music box continued to play and the pocket watch joined in and led them across the attic. They danced around the tables and between the boxes, from one end of the attic to the other.

When Aunt Violet called them down for bed later that night, the Robot King held the children and wouldn't let them go. Lucy said, "We have to go to bed now. We'll be back tomorrow." She and Ezra brought the Robot King over to his table. Lucy kissed him on his cheek. Ezra hugged him one more time and pressed his face into the rosy velvet of the Robot King's coat. He smelled good and felt warm. The pocket watch flew to Ezra, circled him gently, and landed in his pocket.

As the children disappeared through the door in the darkness, they looked back. There was dust falling like bright stars all around the Robot King. They turned away and shut the attic door.

✳

Far away, in the night, there was a *ringing*. It was indistinguishable from the other sounds of the dark at first, but it became louder, and it got closer and closer to the attic. It woke the Robot King up. He sat up and looked out the window.

It was the telephone.

It had returned, ringing and ringing, and it rushed into the attic, followed by the lamp, the radio, and the clock. They were immediately followed by three, ten, thirty, fifty flying pieces of his knees, all the broken pieces that had flown away. They poured through the open window and surrounded the Robot King like a whirl-wind. Then they raced out the window again, and hovered in the air until the Robot King followed. The night was blazing with fireflies and the Robot King watched as they came and formed a long chain behind the flying knees. More and more and more fireflies came until they became a phosphorescent road that stretched from the window, down to the ground, and out into the world.

The Robot King looked back into the attic. A pale green light filled the air. The attic door, with its promise of children, stood locked across the way. The Robot King turned again and looked out the window. The toy train had returned and it chugged in and out of the deep sea of fireflies, which erupted like lava as the train moved through it.

The clock struck midnight as the Robot King stepped through the window. He danced away, down the long shimmering road of fireflies and flying bits of knee, into the shiny lights and flashes of the dark. The pale green glow in the attic faded as the fireflies eventually scattered. But the Robot King had left the window wide open, and it waited for the children, like an invitation.

"HIDE AND SEEK," Lucy said, when she didn't see the Robot King. "Where are you?" She looked around boxes and under the tables and Ezra checked behind the bookshelves. Lucy accidentally knocked over one of her rolling doll heads. It fell on its side and made a loud rattling noise. She and Ezra jumped. The children walked slowly around the attic. It was silent. Lucy bent over to look under a rolled-up rug. "Ezra, help me lift this." There was no answer. "Ezra?" She stood up and saw that Ezra was standing at the open window, looking outside.

The curtains moved and softly touched Ezra's arms. Lucy walked over and stood behind him. She looked out the window too. The sun was very bright.

Ezra walked to the door of the attic. He opened it. "Where are you going?" Lucy said. "Ezra, what's going on?"

He turned back to Lucy and firmly took hold of her hand. He pulled her toward the door. "No, Ezra, stop. He can't be out there, he . . ." Ezra led her down the attic stairs.

When they got to the second floor landing

Lucy tried again to pull away. Ezra held tight.

They passed the locked room that used to be their mother's and made their way down the hall. The carpeting muffled their footsteps. They went down the staircase to the first floor and crept past the back parlor where they heard the clack of shifting pieces as Aunt Violet continued with her giant wooden puzzle.

Ezra opened the big front door. "Would you stop it, Ezra!" Lucy whispered. "Stop it. We locked the attic last night, he can't be—"

Sunlight filled the hall and the children squinted in the brightness. A warm summer wind greeted them as Ezra closed the door silently behind them. Holding tightly to her hand, Ezra brought Lucy down the three brick steps to the stone path.

She looked all around and whispered, "What do we do now?"

Pebbles and leaves crunched beneath their shoes as they made their way across the grass and continued through backyards and crooked streets. Ezra walked slightly ahead of Lucy, but he never let go of her hand. Up ahead there was a very low rumble. As they approached, they began to hear voices and the voices got louder and louder. In a great haze of dust they heard the sounds of trampling feet. Before they knew it, the children were surrounded by what must have been a hundred people, running. The children started running too, as fast as they could.

"Hello? Sir? Why are you running?" Lucy yelled. "Excuse me, ma'am, where is everyone going?"

Just then a hush fell over the crowd and they all stopped running.

There, in the sky, was an old black stove, caught midair and turning. An old woman in an apron was standing in the center of the crowd. There was a long silence as the people watched the stove hover in the sky like a cloud. "That's my stove!" the old woman said. She pointed to the sky and put her hand over her heart. "It's been sitting in my back-yard waiting for the junkman to come and take it away. It never worked a day in its life. *Now* look at it!"

There was a sizzle and a pop and two eggs came flying out of the sky. The old woman caught the eggs in her outstretched apron. The crowd gasped.

"Get me a plate," she screamed. A plate was produced from her house as two long links of sausage sailed down toward her. She flipped the eggs onto the plate, held it out, and caught the sausages as well.

The crowd cheered and yelled.

"Uh-oh," the old woman cried. "Get my teacup, here comes the water!" And a long thin stream of steaming water arched through the air and landed neatly in the old woman's cup. "Thank you," she said to the sky.

And then Lucy knew it was going to be easy to find the Robot King.

"Look," someone in the crowd shouted, "Over there!"

A wild herd of bicycles, of every shape and kind, were pedaling themselves in circles off the ground and into the air. The sky was filled with bicycles. They did somersaults and chased each other across the tree tops.

Ezra and Lucy saw a small shop nearby. The sign in the window read, "Bicycles. Speedy Repairs, Etc." One of the bicycles swooped down right above Ezra and then pulled back into the sky. It came toward the children again, then moved away. The third time, they followed the bicycle away from all the people, down a path to a distant yard where they watched a flock of waffle irons land in a tree. Police sirens wailed all around them. For most of the day, Ezra and Lucy followed the long crooked road of flying things, from one to the next.

As the wild sounds of crowds and machines finally started to die down, an umbrella led them to the edge of a forest. The glint of metal flashed in the leaves. "Ezra, listen . . ."

They heard the sounds of birds fluttering their wings and the sounds of rustling leaves. They heard the silver click of machines hidden in the trees, and from somewhere beneath all that, the children heard a waltz.

They followed the music until they were standing at the doorstep of a small house, deep in the middle of the woods. Ezra knocked on the door. No one answered but the door swung in a little. They waited a few moments, then Ezra pushed the door open and led Lucy into the house—through the kitchen, past the dining room, and down a long hall.

In a small room at the end of the hall, a young woman was sitting at a piano. She faced away from the children, playing the Robot King's waltz. The gold light from a white candle on the piano lit her hair and made it glow. There was a baby in a rocking cradle near her feet, fast asleep. Lucy stared. It all looked so familiar to her somehow. The children listened to the music. Lucy closed her eyes and sighed. As she opened them, the young woman stopped playing and turned around. She was very beautiful.

"Hello," she said gently. "Come and sit

down . . . I'll be right back." She disappeared for a few moments and returned with bread and cakes and two big glasses of milk for the children.

Ezra reached up and touched the young woman's hair. It moved through his fingers and fell again to her shoulders.

"Are you lost?" the young woman asked as they ate.

Lucy shook her head. She wiped off Ezra's milk mustache and then she wiped off her own. "How do you know the Robot King's waltz?" she asked.

The young woman lifted Lucy's face with her hand. "The waltz? Why? Have you heard it before?"

"Yes," said Lucy. Ezra nodded his head vigorously.

"This is strange," the young woman said, "Just a little while ago . . . I really thought it was a dream, or . . ."

"What?" Lucy asked, "What happened?" Ezra moved to the edge of his seat. He rubbed his hands together.

"I was sitting here, rocking my baby to sleep," said the young woman, "when . . . this beautiful green glow came down around the house. It was fireflies, millions of fireflies coming through the branches. And out of this sea of fireflies, I heard music, a waltz. It seemed to hover outside our window, but all I could see was the green light. It played for a long time, right out there, and then it faded, along with the fireflies.

"The baby fell asleep and I carried her to the piano. I found that I knew the tune by heart, so I played it. I thought the whole thing must have been a dream. Isn't that funny? I heard the music so clearly . . . and yet I wasn't even sure if it was real."

Ezra stood up and grabbed the young woman's hand. He was shaking. Then he said, right out loud, "It *was* real!"

Lucy smiled at her brother as tears fell down her cheeks. She squeezed his shoulder. He was still shaking.

"Please," Lucy said to the young woman, "can you tell us which way it went?"

The baby was awake now, laughing in her cradle. Picking her up, the young woman led the children to the back door. She brushed the hair out of Ezra's eyes and kissed him on his cheek. "It seemed to go that way," she said.

They all stepped outside and Ezra pointed up into the trees. "Look!" he said.

A few orange rays from the setting sun burst through the thick leaves. In the fiery glow, a child's rocking horse ducked in and out of the trees above them, followed by a nutcracker, a padlock, and a pewter locket that rushed to the light of the door like a moth. The baby laughed. Everywhere they looked, another flying machine appeared or disappeared through the trees.

"That's the Robot King," Ezra said.

The children hugged the young woman good-bye. "Thank you," Lucy said, and they walked away from her house, hand in hand. Ezra looked back and saw her tightening the blanket around her baby. She took one last look into the trees, and closed the door against the coming night.

Ezra and Lucy headed in the direction the music had gone. They followed the nutcracker, the padlock, and the locket through the woods, like bread crumbs.

THREE

AS THEY MADE their way through the woods, endless waves of dark flowers bloomed all around them and they took off their shoes to run across a stream. Lucy turned to Ezra. "Are you always going to talk," she asked, "or is it just for today?" Ezra looked at his sister. "Always," he promised.

A flying toaster led them over the water. Crickets played their violins. The children stopped to listen. "It's pretty," Ezra said. Lucy nodded. The toaster hovered above them, waiting. It moved again when they did. "I think the machines *want* us to follow them," Lucy said. "They know where he is," Ezra agreed.

The children soon came to the edge of the woods. They stepped into the open. The stars were coming out now and the moon was ready to rise. Everything was blue. The toaster disappeared into a group of machines that seemed to be waiting for the children, outside the woods. The new machines stretched ahead. Lucy and Ezra followed the metallic path as it twisted through fields and between old buildings. The landscape began to look vaguely familiar but they were amazed when, turning the corner of the last building, they found themselves standing alone, at the fallen gates of the old fairgrounds.

The children had never been this close to the fairgrounds before. They looked in the air to see where the flying machines were going to lead them next, but the machines had disappeared.

"Hide and seek," Lucy said to the park. Something howled in the distance as they entered. She tightened her grip on Ezra's hand and shouted, "Hello?"

Her voice echoed back, sounding hollow.

The Ferris wheel swayed high above the children as they searched for the Robot King. Ezra and Lucy climbed through the bones of the roller coaster. The chipped white paint sparkled in the twilight. Wood flapped in the breeze, hitting tin signs, and sand blew against a sea of broken glass. Magnificent towers rose in cracked glory toward the sky. Everything creaked and groaned.

Ezra and Lucy came to the carousel. They looked behind the wooden horses and the old broken seats. The carved animals lay in silence, half covered by weeds and bits of boardwalk.

Ezra and Lucy made their way by moonlight through the park.

"Come home with us," shouted Lucy.

"With us," shouted the echo.

There was only the sound of the wind in the dark. "He's not here," whispered Lucy. "I want to go home."

She was answered by a sudden thunder-

ous *crash*. The carousel exploded with light and started spinning by itself! Lucy screamed as the carved animals heaved and shivered and struggled to escape. As the children ran to the carousel, the Ferris wheel lit up behind them and began to turn. Its engines threw off golden sparks. The children changed direction and ran toward the Ferris wheel, just as all the lights on the towers went on in a giant blaze of electricity. The ground was shaking. Broken bulbs lit up one after another, and became a gigantic drawing in light that raced across the park, outlining everything in gold.

The children ran in desperate circles as Lucy shouted for the Robot King. There was no echo. The sound was swallowed up in the fireworks. In the center of the dazzling blizzard, the children tried to catch their breath.

"I knew he was here," Lucy said.

A thousand metal voices sang from the gears and pulleys of the park. The music grew louder until the children realized that the whole park was waltzing.

And then, like the hand of a giant, the Ferris wheel came and swept the children up, lifting them higher and higher into the night sky.

Ezra watched the park grow small beneath them. They saw the twisting paths that led to their house, and they saw their house itself, away in the distance. The world spread out below them, blinking and burning and opening like a rose. From their seats in the middle of the air, they saw fiery lights ablaze in the north and great storms of electricity skipping brightly across Africa. They saw the oceans rise and fall in silver waves, and now they had a clear view of Paris, the City of Light!

Ezra and Lucy watched as flocks of birds and flying machines swept through the night, sailing in and out of the cities of the earth. The children went higher still.

Ghosts skipped through a misty sea of dreams. Nightmares cracked at the edge of the waters, and a terrible green claw lifted itself out of a wave. The claw turned into stardust and disappeared as the children moved up, out of the dreams. They raised their arms and scraped their fingers across the surface of the moon. They saw Mars and Jupiter. Comets whistled by as the roaring planets moved away, and their house whirled into view once more.

Then, through the night and far away, the children saw their father coming home.

Stars rained down around them as the Ferris wheel, with great care, brought Ezra and Lucy back to the ground.

The light was so bright, they had to cover their eyes. Slowly they made their way to the gates, stepping aside for the carousel animals, which had broken free and were galloping across the fairgrounds. The whole park was breathing fire and the wind felt warm against the children's faces.

Lucy took her brother's hand, and together they stepped out into the dark. Streetlamps blazed on around them, and the children remembered the tiny, make-believe streetlamp of the attic and how they had

danced down the attic road, under the low attic sky.

Ezra and Lucy looked back at the park. The sky arched boundlessly above them.

Ezra took a deep breath. "Good-bye," he said softly.

The children began walking even though they weren't sure which way to go. They could still see the comets speeding by. They could still feel the moon on their fingertips. And they could still hear the waltz of the Robot King's heart.

Suddenly, one of Ezra's pockets opened. Out jumped the pocket watch. It tumbled into the air with a flash of light, and led the children home.